Cat Tales

Rain Cat

Cat Tales

Rain Cat

LINDA NEWBERY

Illustrated by Stephen Lambert

USBORNE

For Zachary

First published in the UK in 2008 by Usborne Publishing Ltd.,
Usborne House, 83-85 Saffron Hill, London EC1N 8RT, England.
www.usborne.com

Text copyright © Linda Newbery, 2008

Illustration copyright © Usborne Publishing Ltd., 2008

A CIP catalogue record for this book is available from the British Library.

JFMAMJJ SOND/08   ISBN 9780746097281   Printed in Great Britain.

Chapter One

It was a summer of hot, hot days, one after another. The sun shone down from a clear blue sky. Jessie could hardly remember when the weather had been any different, though she supposed it must have been, because in her wardrobe there were coats and scarves and gloves, clothes she couldn't imagine ever needing to wear. Now, everyone wore sun hats and sunglasses and sunscreen, and the coolest clothes they could find.

Dad had taken a fortnight off work to spend holiday time with Jessie. Every morning and every evening they went to the allotments, where Dad grew beans, tomatoes, potatoes and peppers. He was very proud of his strip of ground. He'd dug and weeded and raked and planted every bit of it, sometimes helped by Jessie.

After so much dry weather, the plants needed rain.

"Perhaps tomorrow," said Jessie's dad. He and Jessie looked up at the sky, hoping for even the smallest wisp of cloud. "Perhaps the day after. Perhaps next week."

The runner beans were wilting in the heat, the tomatoes thirsting, the peppers turning fire-bright. Dad's face was tomato-red when he carried watering cans to and fro, every morning and every evening. Jessie helped, though the cans were heavy and it was hard not to slosh precious water over her feet.

The water butts had been drained long ago – not a single drop left. Everyone had to use the tap, and there were often queues. Jessie and Dad carried and poured, poured and carried. The baked earth sucked up water in greedy gulps. *More, more,* it gasped. There was never enough. The ground was so dry that cracks opened up.

Jessie pleaded with the sky. "Please rain! Just a little bit! You could, couldn't you?"

It was the same for everyone at the allotments. People had thirsty marrows and peas to look after, callaloo and aubergines, potatoes and carrots, and flowers for cutting. Everyone was busy, growing and tending their fruit and vegetables. Open Day was the week after next, and everyone wanted to grow the plumpest tomatoes, the shiniest onions, the brightest flowers.

"Rain. Rain. Rain." That was Honeysuckle, in the patch next to Dad's, chanting to herself as she weeded her herbs. She saw Jessie looking, and called

across, "We must all think very hard about rain. Think rain and clouds and mist. Think with all your might."

Jessie liked Honeysuckle, with her patchwork waistcoat and tinkling bracelets and smiley face, so she closed her eyes and thought and thought as hard as she could.

She pictured fat, brimming clouds. She heard rain pattering against a window. She saw puddles, saw her feet in wellies, stamping and splashing.

But when she opened her eyes again, the sun was still fierce. It dazzled her, and made her skin prickle.

"Come on, Jessie." Dad was locking up his shed. "Time to go home."

Chapter Two

Next day, the cat was there.

It was lying in the shade of Dad's tool store, on a pile of sacks.

"Oh! Who are you?" Jessie asked.

The cat gazed at her with big, amber eyes. It was an unusual colour – darkest grey, like smoke, like charcoal. It was

the biggest, sleekest, handsomest cat
Jessie had ever seen. She loved cats.
There were two who visited the
allotments, a black one and a stripy
ginger, both from nearby houses. This
one, she was certain, had never been
here before.

She bent to stroke it. The cat turned
its head.

"I wonder who it belongs to?" Dad

bent to look. "No collar. No name tag."

"Whose cat are you?" Jessie asked.
"Where do you come from?"

The cat looked as if it could answer if
it chose to.

"It'll go home soon, I expect," said
Dad. "Come on. Let's start watering."

They'd come early, to water the plants
in the morning cool. The sun was pale
and hazy in the sky. But soon the mist
melted away, and the sun beat down
strongly.

From its pile of sacks,
the cat sat watching. It
licked a paw. It wiped
its whiskers. Dad offered
it water; it looked,
sniffed, then lapped.

A flurry of skirt, trail of scarf, swirl of hair – Honeysuckle was here, with her son, Felix.

"Look!" Jessie pointed to the cat.

Honeysuckle stared. The cat stared back.

"A Rain Cat!" Honeysuckle gasped. "A Royal Rain Cat of Thailand! We must treat him with great respect. He'll bring us good luck. He'll bring us rain."

She bowed to the cat. The cat's eyes, golden as setting suns, gazed back.

"What's a Rain Cat?" Jessie asked.

She'd had a feeling this cat was somehow special, from the way it looked at her when she stroked it.

"See!" Honeysuckle stretched out a hand. "His fur is the darkest, stormiest grey, the colour of rain clouds. This is no ordinary cat. He's a Rain Cat. We must ask him, politely and respectfully, to bring us rain."

Dad stood back, shaking his head. "Go on, then. If you think it'll make the slightest difference. It's a cat. Not a rain god."

Honeysuckle gave him a stern look, then bowed again to the cat. It gave a small sigh.

"Oh, Royal Rain Cat of Thailand—" Honeysuckle began; but stopped. "No. No, not yet. I beg your royal pardon."

"Pardon for what?" Jessie asked. It was hard to keep up with Honeysuckle.

"It's not the proper time. We haven't prepared. We'll do it this evening. A Royal Rain Cat can't be rushed. A Royal Rain Cat shouldn't be sitting on a dusty old sack. We need special food and flowers, and rhymes. Felix, you must make up a poem, and so shall I. Jessie, so must you."

"What sort of poem?"

"A poem about rain, of course."

The cat lowered his eyelids and gave a small sigh, as if all this chatter was keeping him awake.

"A well fed cat like that, he'll have a home to go to," Dad told Honeysuckle. "He'll be gone by evening."

"He won't," said Honeysuckle. "He's come to help. He's come to grant us the favour of rain."

Jessie got on with her watering. It was just one of Honeysuckle's weird ideas, like sowing her seeds by the light of a full moon.

When Jessie and Dad left for home, she took one last look at the cat, in case she didn't see him again later. But she hoped he'd stay.

Inside her a seed of hope was growing.
If the cat was lost, if no one claimed him,
maybe they could take him home, to
keep? She didn't mind if he was a Royal
Rain Cat or not. Just an ordinary cat
would do. A cat of her very own.

Chapter Three

All day long, Jessie struggled with her poem. She thought and wrote, scribbled out, thought and wrote again.

At last she had it. She wasn't sure if this was the kind of poem Honeysuckle wanted, but it was the best she could do. She wrote it out in her best handwriting, with her best ink pen, and decorated it with a border of clouds and rain.

Rain Cat, Rain Cat, be our friend,
Make this baking weather end.
Rain Cat, Rain Cat, good and wise,
Please, please bring us dull grey skies.
Rain Cat, Rain Cat, make it pour.
That's what you're a Rain Cat for.
Rain Cat, Rain Cat, grant our wish.
I will give you nice tinned fish.

That evening, approaching the shed with Dad, Jessie held her breath.

Yes! The cat was still there, blinking on his pile of sacks. He didn't seem to have moved. He studied Jessie with his golden eyes, as if asking what gifts she'd brought him.

When Honeysuckle arrived, she took charge.

"Lotus, Lotus. You're still here. We're so glad." She clasped her hands and bowed deeply.

"Lotus? Is that his name, now?" Jessie asked.

Honeysuckle nodded. "See, the shine on his coat is like dew on a lotus leaf."

Jessie didn't know what a lotus leaf looked like, but it was a nice name.

Honeysuckle had put on a flowing dress, and even more necklaces and bracelets than usual, and had threaded flowers in her hair. She carried a garland of leaves and purple flowers, which she draped around the cat's neck. He didn't seem to mind. Then, taking great care, Honeysuckle lifted him from his pile of

sacks, and carried him underneath the lean-to roof of the shed, where she settled him on a purple velvet cushion, trimmed with silk tassels.

"That's better," she whispered to Jessie. "More suitable for a Royal Rain Cat."

Jessie hadn't dressed up, and neither

had Felix. He grinned at her and rolled his eyes towards the sky. He was used to going along with his mother's strange ideas.

Honeysuckle produced an elegant Chinese saucer, and forked pilchards into it. She offered it to Lotus. He sniffed, paused, then ate, purring a deep, growly purr. Next came a dish of minced chicken.

"Now we must all bow three times, very solemnly. You too," Honeysuckle told Jessie's dad.

The poems came next. Honeysuckle read hers first:

"O Lotus of Thailand,
   Royal Rain Cat,
      Hear our plea.
Cat of clouds, of thunder, of storms,
Bring fruitful rain to this parched earth.
      Beautiful cat,
   Your glossy fur like a moonlit sea,
   Your eyes like blazing sunsets,
   Bring us the blessing of rain."

Next went Jessie, feeling very self-conscious – especially as other allotmenteers had started to gather and listen. Some began to laugh, until Honeysuckle glared at them.

Lastly, Felix. His poem was simple:

"Rain, rain,
Pour, pour,
Rain, rain,
And rain some more."

They all stood in a semicircle, looking at Lotus.

He didn't look impressed. He didn't even look interested. He just flicked an ear, blinked twice and went to sleep.

"That's that, then," said Dad. "Come on, Jessie. There's watering to be done."

Chapter Four

Next morning, waking up, Jessie
listened and listened.

Something was different.

It was a sound she hadn't heard for a
very long time. Rain battering the
window! She was out of bed at once,
pulling back the curtains.

YES!

Grey, dull sky.

Lashing rain.

Puddles.

Wet shiny road.

She did a handstand of pure joy, then heard Dad calling, "Jessie! It's raining! Really raining!"

"I know!"

As soon as she was dressed, Jessie called to Dad that she had to go outside for a minute. Down in the lift she went, to stand outside the main door of the flats – holding out her hands, opening her mouth, getting wet. Rain! Real rain!

She felt so energetic, after all that heat, that she bounded back up the six flights of stairs.

"It's just a coincidence," Dad said while they had breakfast. "That cat didn't have anything to do with it. Still, we can have a rest from watering for once."

But of course they had to go to the
allotment to see if Lotus was still there.

Yes, he was. He was sitting on his
velvet cushion, under the lean-to roof.
Did he look a bit smug? A bit pleased
with himself? Jessie felt sure he did.

She and Dad had bought tinned cat
food and a packet of biscuits on the way,
but Honeysuckle had got there first, with
wafer-thin chicken and Gourmet Cat
Minced Morsels. And cream. Lotus ate
the lot, purring his growly purr.

"Lotus! Wonderful Rain Cat! I knew
you'd do it," she gushed. "Thank you,
thank you!"

Other allotmenteers had come,
huddled into raincoats, sheltering
under umbrellas, for the sheer
pleasure of seeing the ground sucking
down wetness, of hearing the *blip-blip-
blop* as water dripped into the butts,
of seeing the shine on tomatoes and
leaves. It seemed the earth was
sighing with pleasure.

"What about Lotus now, though,
Dad?" Jessie asked on the way home.
"What will we do? Can we keep him?"

Dad looked doubtful. "Well, I don't
know. I wouldn't mind having a cat,
but he's a bit of a *special* cat, isn't he?
He must belong to someone. I'll put
up notices, and phone the vets and
the RSPCA."

"And then? If no one claims him?"

"We'll see."

We'll see! That was nearly as good as *Yes*, wasn't it, in Dad-speak? Jessie's hopes soared, and she crossed her fingers tightly.

But when they got back home, and she looked around their flat, she wasn't sure it was the right sort of place for a Royal Rain Cat. Lotus was the kind of cat who expected *luxury*. Still, at least he was a grown-up cat, not a kitten – Dad said, whenever Jessie asked, that they couldn't keep a kitten in a sixth-floor flat.

"It wouldn't be fair, shutting a lively kitten indoors. You'll be back at school soon, and it'd be alone all day. And we couldn't even let it out on the balcony in case it fell off."

Lotus didn't look like the kind of cat who'd skitter about and fall off a balcony. In fact, as the days went by, Jessie hardly saw him do anything at all. He just sat on his cushion, and stared, and ate. When the rain eased a little, he went for a stroll around the allotments, proud and dignified as a king surveying his realm.

Then he went back to his cushion to
lick himself dry and preen his whiskers.
Could he be Jessie's cat? Would he?

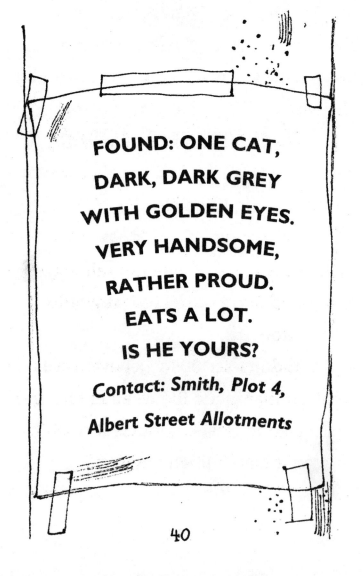

**FOUND: ONE CAT,
DARK, DARK GREY
WITH GOLDEN EYES.
VERY HANDSOME,
RATHER PROUD.
EATS A LOT.
IS HE YOURS?**
Contact: Smith, Plot 4,
Albert Street Allotments

Chapter Five

Three days later it was still raining.
It poured and poured as if it would
never stop.

"You don't seriously believe it was
that cat that made the weather change?"
Felix said to Jessie. "Course it wasn't.
It would have rained anyway."

The allotmenteers had been pleased at first, but now their tender seedlings were battered, their flowers flattened, their polytunnels awash. And still it rained.

In ones and twos, they came to Honeysuckle, in their raincoats and their muddy wellingtons.

"You did this! You and that cat. Can't you tell him to make it stop?"

"Enough's enough! This is like monsoon season."

"My shed's going to float away if it rains much more."

Honeysuckle sat under her umbrella, and had a think.

"All right. We'll have another ceremony. Felix, Jessie – you must each write another poem. We'll thank Lotus

very nicely and politely for the rain, but
ask for dry weather now."

Jessie struggled some more with paper,
pencil and words. This time Dad
helped, though he treated the whole
thing as a joke.

At last, between them, they'd written:

Thank you, thank you for the rain!
But could you make it stop?
This poem is to ask you for
Another weather swap.
Please don't think we're ungrateful.
It was very nice at first
For all our veg and flowers
To forget the heat and thirst.
But now it's poured and poured so much
They don't know which is worse.
So thank you for the lovely rain,
Every single drop,
But now that we're all soaking,
Could you kindly make it stop?

Jessie wrote it out, decorated it with beaming sun faces, then scrolled it up and tied it with string.

Next day, a damp procession, faces hidden under hoods and umbrellas, tramped and splashed towards Lotus.

Under the lean-to roof he was quite dry. Honeysuckle had brought a wooden stool from home, and had placed the velvet cushion on the seat, so Lotus now seemed to survey them all from a throne.

Today she'd brought sardines in a bone-china bowl, and Felix carried a dish of cream. In Jessie's opinion, Lotus was eating far too much for a cat who did nothing but sit on a cushion. She'd bought him a catnip mouse – even though Lotus was far too dignified to play with a toy.

He licked the saucers clean, washed his paws and whiskers, then settled down to rest.

Honeysuckle stepped forward with a new flower garland. The hem of her frilly dress trailed soggily over her wellingtons as she draped the flowers around Lotus's neck. The cat took no notice at all as she recited her poem

"O Royal Cat, in your wisdom
You have blessed us with healing rain,
Till the leaves burst forth anew
And the streams burble.
Now please in your wisdom,
send us balmy days of sunshine,
With soft breezes
That whisper of your greatness."

She stepped back. "Go on, Jessie. Your turn."

Jessie read fast enough to reach the end before the rain turned the paper to mush.

"Now Felix..."

"Okay, you've made your point
With all the rainy stuff.
But after four whole days of it
Enough, enough, enough!"

Jessie giggled. Lotus opened one eye, closed it again, then gave a small snore.

Felix gave her a nudge. "He's not listening. He's asleep."

"Never underestimate the power of a Royal Rain Cat," Honeysuckle told them. "Have faith. Tomorrow will be different."

Jessie didn't really believe it, and Dad and Felix certainly didn't.

There wasn't much of an audience today – only the few allotmenteers who had ventured out, and were sheltering under their lean-to roofs with flasks of coffee or hot soup.

Still it rained. It rained and it rained and it rained.

Chapter Six

Waking up, Jessie listened very carefully to what was happening outside.

Wind. High wind.

She jumped out of bed, pulled back the curtains and looked out.

Huffing, tumbling, gusting wind.

Papers and cartons bowling along the pavement.

Trees tossing and writhing.

A few brave birds trying to fly.

But it wasn't raining. The sky was bright, flecked with scudding clouds.

Dad and Jessie, leaning into the wind, set off after breakfast to see what Lotus was doing, and what Honeysuckle had to say.

Jessie was anxious. "Perhaps Lotus thought we weren't grateful enough. Perhaps we weren't very polite."

"Jess!" Dad tweaked her ponytail. "You know this is nonsense really, don't you? It's just pretending. That cat can't control the weather. How could he?"

"I know," Jessie said, but her voice sounded doubtful, even to herself. The way Lotus looked at her! He knew more than he was letting on. He was a wise and clever cat, without doubt.

Honeysuckle had asked for breezes, hadn't she? And breezes were breezing today, for sure. It felt like the end of summer.

Jessie would be back at school the week after next, and so would Felix, and Dad would be at work all day. Autumn would come soon, then winter. What would happen to Lotus? They couldn't leave him sitting on his throne, all through the cold weather and the dark days.

Jessie asked the question aloud. "Shall we keep him? Bring him home?"

"I knew you'd ask that. I'm not sure he's the right cat for us," said Dad. "And

I'm not sure we're the right people for *him*."

At the allotments, everyone was busy – putting in new stakes to stop the runner beans from blowing away, gathering up wind-blown pots, tying down their polytunnels. Jessie helped for a while, then went to look at Lotus. As usual, he sat blinking and gazing from his cushion. Glossy and sleek, he surveyed everyone like a king looking at his subjects. Jessie thought he was getting fatter and fatter.

She soon realized why. Other people, not just Honeysuckle, had started bringing gifts of food and flowers, poems they'd written and pictures they'd drawn.

They wrote notes asking for better weather, or for favours, or wishes granted. The ground by the throne was strewn with flowers, gifts, and dishes licked to a glossy shine.

Perhaps Dad was right, about Lotus not being the cat for them. He was a bit haughty, a bit aloof. Jessie wanted an ordinary cat, a cat to cuddle and play with.

This gave her an idea.

In secret, at home, she worked hard on a new poem:

Lotus of the smoky fur,
Golden eyes and growly purr,
Here's a small request for you.
Is there something you can do?

We live in a sixth–floor flat,
But all the same I'd like a cat,
A pet to call my very own,
Not a kitten, but full–grown.
A cat that likes to stay indoors,
Watch TV and wash her paws.
I'd buy a collar and a bell,
And care for her extremely well.
We'd go for health checks at the vet –
I'd make a note, and not forget.
We'd play with toys and bits of string.
I'd love her more than anything,
My little cat with tabby fur –
I dream and dream and dream of her.
I'd give her cat food twice a day,
I'd clean and scrub her litter tray,
And not mind if it's messy.
Thanks for listening. Jessie x

Chapter Seven

Next morning, while Dad was busy weeding, Jessie crouched beside Lotus's throne and whispered her poem into his ear.

She felt a bit silly. When she'd finished, he looked at her hard, opened his mouth in a huge yawn, and shut it again with a snap, as if announcing that something should be done.

But he wasn't doing very well with the weather. The wind had dropped, but today was grey and dull. Everyone wanted sun again, for a last burst of ripening before Open Day. Honeysuckle had asked Lotus for sun, and so had lots of other people, bringing titbits of chicken and fish and cat biscuits. He scoffed everything he was given, sat on his cushion and stared, and nothing changed. People began to doubt that he'd ever done anything at all.

Felix was triumphant. "See? Sometimes it rains and sometimes it doesn't, that's all."

"He's a mysterious cat," Jessie said. "He does things his own way. He won't be told what to do."

"He knows we're all suckers, that's what," said Felix. "Specially Mum."

Honeysuckle was Lotus's loyal supporter. "He's used up all his power, granting our requests. He needs to rest. Recharge."

"Prove it," said Felix.

Honeysuckle was removing faded flowers from Lotus's garland. "I don't need *proof*. Proof is for people with no faith. You wait and see. He'll give us good weather for Open Day."

Now that she'd read him her secret poem, Jessie really did want to believe that Lotus could make things happen. She gave him a special, private look.

She might have imagined it, but she thought he winked.

Saturday, Open Day, saw a return to
bright sunny weather – not *too* hot, not
unbearable, just a perfect August day,
with the slightest of breezes.

So those (like Honeysuckle) who
wanted to believe in the Rain Cat said

that Lotus had made it happen, and those (like Felix and Dad) who didn't, said that the weather was good because the weather was good.

Jessie hoped.

Everyone was busy – putting up signs outside, setting up displays, handing out badges, getting raffle prizes ready. Jessie and Dad's produce stall was already heaped with tomatoes, onions, lettuces, beans, peppers, spinach, courgettes and radishes. Next to them, Honeysuckle's table was loaded with pots of herbs. Nearby, four cooks were making kebabs, fritters and pies. Jessie's stomach was rumbling already. Flags fluttered by the entrance gate.

Every allotment was neat, tidy and

perfectly weeded. The soil was not too wet, not too dry – it was just right.

People started to arrive. The steel band played, and the cooks cooked, and the sun shone.

"O thank you, Royal Rain Cat, for this blessing of perfect weather." Honeysuckle bowed double in front of Lotus's throne, and backed away from his royal presence.

Lotus was the star attraction.

"He's a Royal Rain Cat of Thailand," Honeysuckle told everyone. "No ordinary cat. *Oh* no. It's thanks to him we had such good rain when we needed it."

Some of the visitors looked impressed. Others looked at Honeysuckle as if she were mad. But everyone looked at Lotus with the greatest admiration and respect. Lots of the visitors took his photo. In return, he gave them his haughtiest stare.

"He's here to stay," Felix told Jessie. "Part of the place. There's nothing for it – we'll have to build him a palace. And be his servants for ever."

She giggled. "Aren't we already?"

Then a loud voice rose above all
the others.

"FRED! Mum – there's FRED!"

Chapter Eight

The voice belonged to a black-haired
boy, a bit younger than Jessie and Felix.

"Fred! That's my Fred!" he shouted
again, and burst into tears.

It was Lotus he was pointing at. Lotus
stared, and gave a tiny miaow, and even
moved to the front edge of his throne.

The boy's mother stopped dead. "Is it? It IS! Our Fred!"

They came closer. Their eyes were big and round, fixed on Lotus's amber ones. They both stared, and Lotus stared back.

"Yes! That's Fred all right. Oh, thank goodness," said the mum. "Where did you find him?" she asked Honeysuckle.

"He wandered off ten days ago – we searched and searched. We'd almost given up hope! Careful, Ben. We don't want him to run away again."

The boy gathered Lotus up, a heavy armful, and buried his face in the cat's thick fur.

"*Fred?*" said Honeysuckle. "This is *Lotus*. He's a Royal Rain Cat of Thailand, you know."

"He isn't." The mum shook her head. "He's our Fred. A daft old haddock."

"We thought we'd never see him again," sniffed Ben, through a faceful of fur.

"He's chosen to come and live here," said Honeysuckle.

"But he's *ours*."

Honeysuckle and the mum stood sizing each other up.

Jessie edged closer. She knew Honeysuckle wouldn't want to part with her Royal Rain Cat. Not to someone who called him Fred. But Lotus recognized them; Jessie had seen that. He *must* be theirs.

Dad stepped forward. "Let's all sit down, and decide what to do."

He bought drinks for everyone – tea for the grown-ups, juice for Jessie, Ben and Felix, and carrot cake all round.

Honeysuckle jutted her chin at the mum. "He's your cat, you say? Prove it."

"No problem." The mum reached into her bag and took out a mobile phone. She clicked to a photo, showed Honeysuckle, then showed it to all of them in turn. It was Ben, in a kitchen, big smile on his face, cuddling Lotus just as he was cuddling him now.

Lotus – yes, it was him for sure – gazed at the camera, his eyes like golden lamps.

Honeysuckle swallowed, and nodded.

"And if you care to check, you'll find that Fred's got three white hairs on his tummy," added the mum.

The cat met Jessie's eye, then looked away. She might almost have thought he was embarrassed at being found out. Her heart thudded with disappointment. He was just Fred, then. Not a Rain Cat with special powers. It had been pointless, asking him for favours.

"Thank you for looking after him," said the mum. "You must have, er, fed him very well – he's put on weight. You big porky," she told the cat.

Yes, Lotus/Fred definitely looked ashamed now.

"We'll go home for the cat-carrier, and come straight back. We're only three streets away." The mum brushed cake crumbs off her lap. "Come on, Ben. Put him back on his cushion. Could you keep an eye on him?" she asked Dad. "Make sure he doesn't run off again? Thanks for the tea and cake."

"See?" said Felix, when they'd gone. "I told you he was just a cat. Huh! Pretending to be a Royal Rain Cat! He's just a fat old moggy. What a fake!"

"You can't blame *him* for that!" Jessie protested.

Honeysuckle had gone silent. She removed Lotus/Fred's garland, and tidied the food dishes.

Was it Jessie's imagination, or did Lotus/Fred already look more ordinary – smaller, less glossy?

Ben and his mum were soon back, with their cat-carrier. It was only just big enough. Lotus/Fred looked a bit offended as he was stuffed in. Then he folded his paws and sat comfortably.

"Bye, Lotus," Jessie said sadly. "Fred, I mean."

"He's heavy to carry. Let me walk round with you," Dad offered. "You can look after the stall for a few minutes, can't you, Jess?"

Jessie nodded, and watched the three of them set off towards the gate, Dad in the middle with the carrier.

Lotus/Fred turned his head and gave her a last look.

Did he give just the hint of a wink?

No, she must have imagined it.

It seemed all wrong without him. Jessie served customers with tomatoes and beans, but every time the stall went quiet she looked at the empty throne, the abandoned cushion, the discarded flowers. She saw Honeysuckle doing the same. Still, Lotus/Fred had gone to his own home, and they ought to be glad.

Chapter Nine

The Open Day had been a big success, even with Lotus gone.

Dad was looking very pleased with himself as he and Jessie walked home.

"We need to go shopping tomorrow," he told her.

"Shopping? For what?" Jessie knew

that Dad *hated* shopping.

"We need a cat basket, and a litter tray, and some toys, and tins of cat food."

"*What?*" Jessie couldn't believe her ears. "Is Lotus coming to live with us after all?"

"Not Lotus."

"Who, then? Fred?"

Dad smiled. "Not Fred either. Here's what I found out when I walked home with Ben and his mum. They've had Fred for three years, and he's rather a special cat, as we know. *Not* because he's got magical powers, or can make it rain, or anything like that. Just because he's a lovely cat."

"A lovely, gorgeous cat," agreed Jessie.

"Well, a month ago they adopted another one, a little cat that needed a home because its owner was going abroad. They've got quite a big house, so they thought the new cat would fit in easily, but the problem was that Fred was jealous. Went into a huge sulk. Wouldn't speak to them, wouldn't purr, wouldn't play. Hissed at this poor little cat whenever he saw it. And then he left home altogether."

"That's when he came to the allotments?" Jessie asked.

Dad nodded. "That's right. They expected him to come back, Ben and his mum, because he'd never wandered before. When he didn't, they searched everywhere. And now they've found him."

"So everything's all right?" said Jessie, not quite seeing.

"Not really. Problem is, as soon as we let Fred out of his basket, he saw this little cat and flew into a rage again. Chased it under the sofa. Hissed and growled. And Ben's mum said, oh dear, she could see trouble ahead, she wished they hadn't taken in this other cat.

It's not fair to Fred, when he's used to being on his own. And they don't want him to wander off again."

He looked at Jessie and grinned.

"So, yes?" She tugged at his arm. "*Then* what?"

"So," said Dad, "I told Ben's mum, *I* know someone who'd like a little cat, a grown-up cat, a cat that's used to being indoors. I know someone who'd look after it and love it and give it the best home in the world—"

Jessie bounced on the spot. "You mean *me*! You mean *us*!"

"That's right. So, tomorrow, when we're ready, we'll go and collect Tabitha."

"Tabitha! Is she—"

"Tabby, yes. A pretty tabby cat."

"A little cat of my own! Exactly the cat I wanted. Clever, clever Lotus! Clever Fred!"

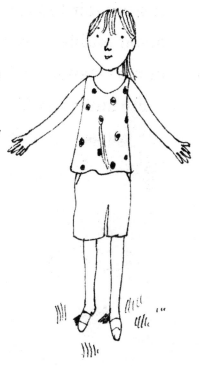

Had he known, she wondered? Was that why he winked?

Whether it was his doing or not, Jessie was about to get the best present she could think of. And Lotus/Fred was getting what *he* wanted, too.

She was full of energy. She hopscotched along the pavement as far as the park wall, then jumped up and tightrope-walked all the way along to the gates, then ran to the grass and turned six cartwheels of pure delight.

Tabitha! A cat of her very own!

She couldn't wait.

Tabby and Jessie. Jessie and Tabby.

Jessie knows that she's got the best cat in the world. And Tabby knows that she's got the best owner in the world.

Jessie does all the things she promised. She feeds Tabby twice a day. She takes her to the vet. She cleans the litter tray. She rolls ping-pong balls and dangles bits of string for Tabby to pounce at.

Tabby doesn't mind staying in, because she's always been an indoors cat.

Dad's bought a
special cat harness,
and sometimes Jessie
takes her for walks
outside on the
grass, like a dog.

She can't imagine that Lotus/Fred
would agree to that, but Tabby doesn't
mind at all.

Sometimes it's sunny, and sometimes
it rains. And when Jessie looks out of

the rain-spattered window, she thinks of
Lotus, the Rain Cat, with his storm-grey
fur and his eyes like shining lanterns,
and she wonders if he had anything to
do with it.

Or maybe he's just Fred, snoring on a
cushion, as cats do.

About the author

Linda Newbery loves to write. She also loves her four cats: Holly, Hazel, Finn and Fleur who keep her busy and who have inspired Cat Tales. Linda had her first novel published in 1988 and she's the author of many books for young readers. She has won the Silver Medal Nestlé Children's Book Prize and the Costa Children's Book Award.

Linda writes in a hut in her garden, usually with a cat or two for company.

Cat Tales

Curl up with Cat Tales from award-winning and enchanting storyteller, Linda Newbery.

The Cat with Two Names

Two of everything sounds perfect, but it soon leads to double the trouble for Cat...

ISBN 9780746096147

Rain Cat

Nobody believes that the mysterious cat can control the weather...until it starts to rain!

ISBN 978074609728

And coming soon...

Smoke Cat

Where do the shadowy cats in next door's garden come from and why won't one particular cat join them?

ISBN 9780746097298

Shop Cat

Strange things have started happening in the toy shop since Twister came to stay...

ISBN 9780746097304

Ice Cat

Tom's cat is made of snow and ice, so of course it can't come alive...or can it?

ISBN 9780746097311

All priced at £3.99

For more fun and furry
animal stories, log on to
www.fiction.usborne.com

The Pony-Mad Princess

by Diana Kimpton

Princess Ellie to the Rescue
Can Ellie save her beloved pony, Sundance, when
he goes missing?   ISBN 9780746060186

Princess Ellie's Secret
Ellie comes up with a secret plan to stop Shadow
from being sold.   ISBN 9780746060193

A Puzzle for Princess Ellie
Why won't Rainbow go down the spooky
woodland path?   ISBN 9780746060209

Princess Ellie's Starlight Adventure
Hoofprints appear on the palace lawn and Ellie
has to find the culprit.   ISBN 9780746060216

Princess Ellie's Moonlight Mystery
Ellie is enjoying pony camp, until she hears noises
in the night.   ISBN 9780746060223

A Surprise for Princess Ellie
Ellie sets off in search of adventure, but ends up
with a big surprise.   ISBN 9780746060230

Princess Ellie's Holiday Adventure
Ellie and Kate go to visit Prince John, and get lost
in the snow!   ISBN 9780746067321

Princess Ellie and the Palace Plot
Can Ellie's pony, Starlight, help her uncover the
palace plot?   ISBN 9780746067338

Princess Ellie's Christmas
Ellie's plan for the perfect Christmas present goes
horribly wrong...   ISBN 9780746068335

Princess Ellie Saves the Day
Can Ellie save the day when one of her ponies
gets ill?   ISBN 9780746068342

Princess Ellie's Summer Holiday
Wilfred the Wonder Dog is missing and it's up to
Ellie to find him.   ISBN 9780746073087

Princess Ellie's Secret Treasure Hunt
Will Ellie finds the secret treasure buried in the
palace grounds?   ISBN 9780746085745